A NOTE TO PARENTS

When your children are ready to "step into reading," giving them the right books—and lots of them—is as crucial as giving them the right food to eat. **Step into Reading Books** present exciting stories and information reinforced with lively, colorful illustrations that make learning to read fun, satisfying, and worthwhile. They are priced so that acquiring an entire library of them is affordable. And they are beginning readers with an important difference—they're written on four levels.

Step 1 Books, with their very large type and extremely simple vocabulary, have been created for the very youngest readers. **Step 2 Books** are both longer and slightly more difficult. **Step 3 Books,** written to mid-second-grade reading levels, are for the child who has acquired even greater reading skills. **Step 4 Books** offer exciting nonfiction for the increasingly proficient reader.

Children develop at different ages. **Step into Reading Books,** with their four levels of reading, are designed to help children become good—and interested—readers *faster.* The grade levels assigned to the four steps—preschool through grade 1 for Step 1, grades 1 through 3 for Step 2, grades 2 and 3 for Step 3, and grades 2 through 4 for Step 4—are intended only as guides. Some children move through all four steps very rapidly; others climb the steps over a period of several years. These books will help your child "step into reading" in style!

Library of Congress Cataloging in Publication Data: Hayward, Linda. Noah's ark. (Step into reading. A Step 1 book)
SUMMARY: A simple retelling of the Old Testament story of Noah, who followed God's orders to build a great ark
in preparation for the coming flood. 1. Noah's ark—Juvenile literature. [1. Noah (Biblical figure) 2. Noah's ark.
3. Bible stories—O.T.] I. Wright, Freire, ill. II. Title. III. Series: Step into reading. Step 1 book. BS658.H43   1987
222′.1209505   86-17790   ISBN: 0-394-88716-6 (trade); 0-394-98716-0 (lib. bdg.)

Step into Reading

Noah's Ark

A Story from the Bible

Adapted by Linda Hayward
Illustrated by Freire Wright

A Step 1 Book

Random House New York

Manufactured in the United States of America

18 19 20

Noah lived long ago.
He was a good man.
He listened to God.

God told Noah
to build an ark.

And Noah did.
He made it big
and strong
and long
and wide.

He made a window
at the top.
He made a door
in the side.

God told Noah
to put food
in the ark.
And Noah did.

He put in hay
and seeds
and fruits
and vegetables.

God told Noah
to take animals
into the ark.
And Noah did.

He took in two
of every kind.

He took in frogs

and lizards

and birds

and beetles.

He took in camels

and bears

and lions

and monkeys.

In they went,
through the door.

In they went,
two by two.

God told Noah
to bring in
his family.
And Noah did.

He brought in
his wife
and his sons
and his sons' wives
and his grandchildren.

God said:
"I will send
a great flood.
It will rid
the world
of wickedness."

Noah watched
the rain
begin to fall.

The rain fell   for forty days

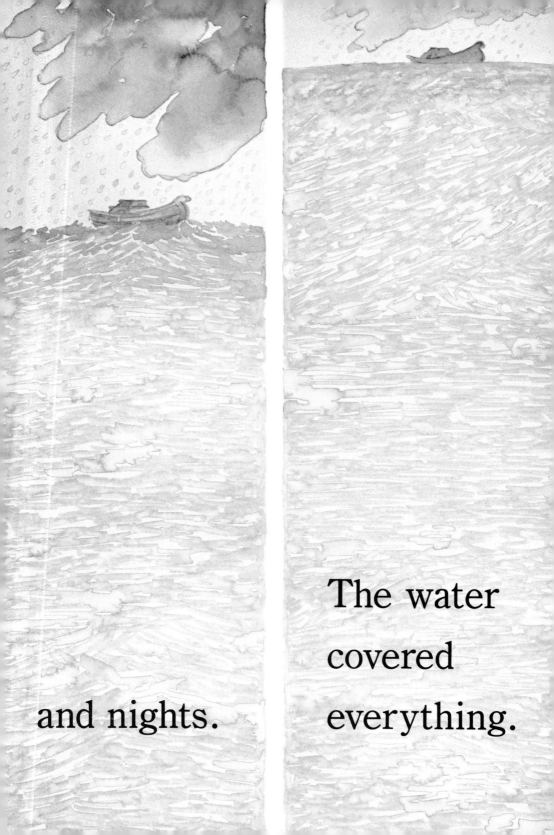

and nights.

The water
covered
everything.

Noah's ark
floated
on the water.

Everyone
inside the ark
was saved.

Then God
sent a wind.
The wind
dried up
the water.

The ark
came to rest.

Noah sent out
a dove.

The dove
came back
with a twig.

Everyone wanted
to go outside.
But Noah waited.

Then one day
Noah opened
the door.

The sun was shining.
Out came the animals,
two by two.

Noah looked up.
He saw a great
rainbow
in the sky.

Then God said:
''I will never
send a great
flood again.''

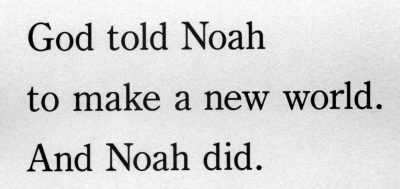

God told Noah
to make a new world.
And Noah did.